PB

BROTHERS AND SISTERS

by Rob Lewis

British Library Cataloguing in Publication Data
A catalogue record of this book is available from
the British Library.
ISBN 0 340 86600 4 (HB)
ISBN 0 340 86601 2 (PB)

First edition published 2004
10 9 8 7 6 5 4 3 2 1

Published by Hodder Children's Books
a division of Hodder Headline Limited
338 Euston Road London NW1 3BH

Printed in China

BROTHERS AND SISTERS

ROB LEWIS

Hodder
Children's
Books

A division of Hodder Headline Limited

Brothers are trouble. Sisters are too!

Brothers like leaping around.

Sisters like playing tricks.

Brothers like scribbling,

on toys and on walls.

Sisters are messy, splashing water
on the floor.

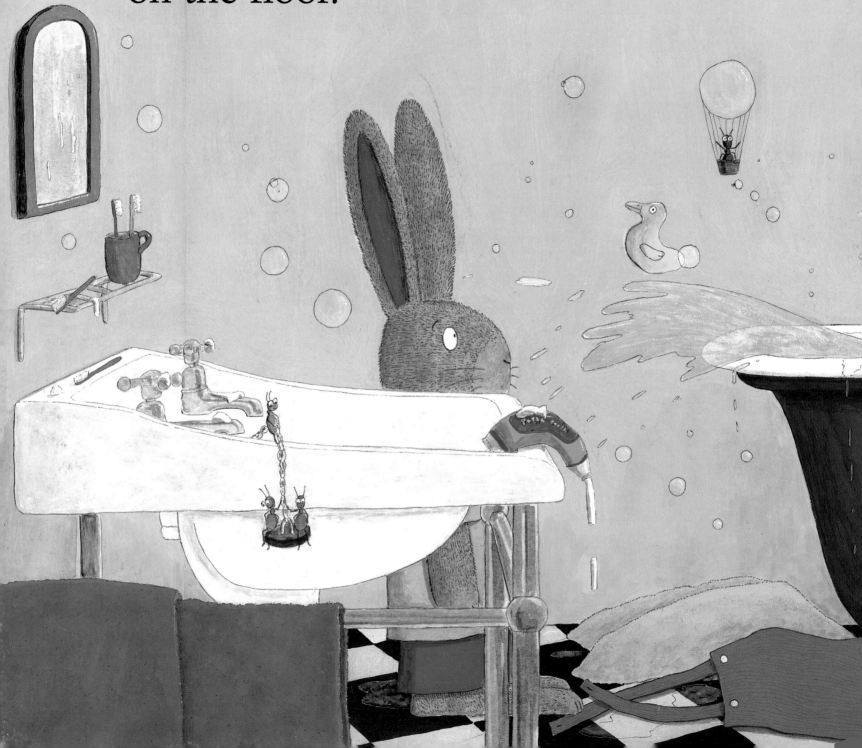

Brothers put you off your food.

Sisters like to be the boss.

But... brothers also make you laugh.

Sisters are good at throwing.

Brothers help you

to be brave.

Sisters are good to share storms with.

Brothers and sisters make a great team.

And when you're feeling lonely,
you can be best friends.

We are!